Stewie Scraps

and the

Star Rocket

Written by Sheila M Blackburn
and illustrated by Leighton Noyes

Brilliant Publications

Brilliant Publications
www.brilliantpublications.co.uk

Sales Office
BEBC (Brilliant Publications)
Albion Close, Parkstone, Poole, Dorset, BH12 3LL, UK
Tel: 01202 712910
Fax: 0845 1309300
e-mail: brilliant@bebc.co.uk

Editorial Office
Unit 10, Sparrow Hall Farm
Edlesborough
Dunstable, Bedfordshire, LU6 2ES, UK
Tel: 01525 222292
e-mail: info@brilliantpublications.co.uk

The name 'Brilliant Publications' and the logo are registered trade marks.

Written by Sheila M Blackburn.
Cover illustration and inside illustrations by Leighton Noyes.

© Sheila M Blackburn 2007

ISBN numbers:

Stewie Scraps and the …		
	Star Rocket	978-1-903853-87-0
	Space Racer	978-1-903853-84-9
	Easy Rider	978-1-903853-85-6
	Giant Joggers	978-1-903853-86-3
	Trolley Cart	978-1-903853-88-7
	Super Sleigh	978-1-903853-89-4

Set of 6 books ISBN 978-1-903853-90-0
6 sets of 6 books ISBN 978-1-903853-91-7

First printed by Dardedze Holography in Latvia in 2008
10 9 8 7 6 5 4 3 2 1

The right of Sheila Blackburn to be identified as the author of this work has been asserted by herself in accordance with Copyright, Design and Patents Act 1988.

If you would like further information on any of our other titles, or to request a catalogue, please visit our website www.brilliantpublications.co.uk

Contents

For Janet, who loved fireworks and would have loved Stewie, and with thanks and love to Tom.

A huge thank you "to everyone at Brilliant Publications and especially to Priscilla Hannaford".

Remember the 5th of November

November.

Dull, dark and dreary, the days seemed to go on forever. The October half-term holiday was over and Stewie Scraps found himself back at school, living for Fridays and Mr Melling's craft lessons. He'd even found a use for all that number work in his maths lessons – to work out how many days till the next school holidays.

5

"Cheer up!" Grandpa said to Stewie one evening. "It's only seven weeks till Christmas. Do you want me to tell you how many shopping days left?"

Stewie looked hard at Grandpa. Sometimes he had the strangest ideas. Shopping days till Christmas? Why on Earth would Stewie Scraps be interested in shopping? Why shop when you could simply *make* what you wanted instead?

"Well, anyway," Grandpa went on, "there's always Bonfire Night — all those fireworks. You still like fireworks, don't you, Stewie?"

Stewie shrugged.

What was the point of getting interested in Bonfire Night? He knew that Flo and JJ would be too busy to take him to see any fireworks. His big sister, Poppy, would be organizing her latest boyfriend to take her to a flash fireworks display. And Clint would just jump on his bike at the last minute and head off into the night in his old black-leather jacket.

For some years, JJ and Grandpa had
tried. They had let off a few little fireworks
in the yard behind the shop, but they were
never up to much.

"Damp squibs, dearie," Flo said. "Total
waste of time and money."

9

"Well, the thing is," Grandpa said to Stewie, "there's to be a bit of a fireworks do at the pub on Friday in the garden at the back. They want to try something different for charity. You could come with me, Stewie, for some pop and crisps and some big bangers."

Stewie shrugged again and said he'd think about it. He went back to drawing in his secret design book.

Projectile project

At last, Friday came – the 5th of November.

And eventually it was time for the craft lesson.

Stewie was keen. He pushed his way into the room to see what they would be doing … and was met by nothing. No tools, no equipment, no kits for constructing things.

Nothing.

Trust grown-ups to let you down like that!

Mr Melling sat at his desk when all the children had gathered. He put his fingertips together like a tent and looked as if he had something important to say.

Stewie waited.

12

Mr Melling looked very serious. He said that they were going to do some work about joining things together today. The new project was going to be about different ways to join things and make hinges.

Stewie liked the sound of this. It could come in useful in some of his own designs back at home.

"But," Mr Melling went on with his serious face, "the stock has not arrived yet. The order has been made, but we are still waiting for the things to be delivered. So, this week instead," he smiled, "as it's Bonfire Night, I'd like you to design a new firework."

Yes! If a new firework design was what Mr Melling wanted, then a very new and amazing firework design was what he was going to get!

14

It took Stewie the rest of the lesson and the first part of afternoon playtime to produce his Super Star Rocket design. He used only the best drawing pencils, absolutely no felt tips and a lot of very detailed labels.

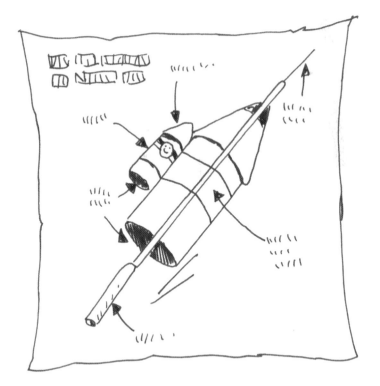

"And what have we here?" Mr Melling asked standing behind Stewie and looking down rather puzzled.

"A Super Star Rocket, Sir – with side passenger pod."

Mr Melling put down his tea and picked up Stewie's piece of paper with the labelled design.

It was rare for Stewie Scraps to write so many words.

"A passenger pod? A little dangerous, perhaps?"

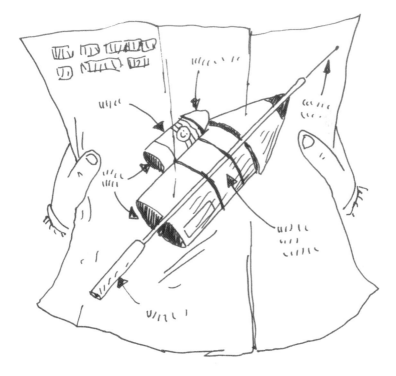

"No, Sir," Stewie answered. "Not if you wear the correct down-suit and stick to the rules."

"A down-suit?" said Mr Melling.

"Yes, Sir. The passenger rides in the pod on the side of the rocket. It goes up and up and, before it explodes, the pod bursts and the passenger floats gently back to Earth in his special down-suit — it acts a bit like a parachute and it's very safe."

"And why would you want to do that?"

Stewie grinned.

"To be part of that great starburst and all that colour, Sir. A great experience."

Mr Melling snorted and finished his tea.

Ooooooh! – Aaaaaah!

That evening, Stewie and Grandpa picked a good seat in the garden at the back of the pub. It wasn't really a garden as such – just a few concrete slabs and some old plastic chairs and tables that they'd bought off JJ.

Muffled up against the night air in a bobble hat and woolly scarf, Stewie was happy to sit near the rocket launcher and be fed lots and lots of pop and crisps and then burgers from the barbecue.

The oil-drum barbecue fascinated Stewie, but not as much as the rocket launcher. It was made of thick, wooden fence posts, lashed together at the right launching angle. Stewie made a mental note of it for his secret design book. It would be useful, too, for Mr Melling's craft work on joining.

Soon it was time for the fireworks. Some were big, loud bangers that shook the ground. Others were great, whizzing wheels with trails of spikey white lights, or fountains of tumbling fire that whooshed and spat into the ground. And then there were the rockets.

Stewie had never seen such big rockets before. It took Grandpa's mate, Fred, a lot of effort to lift each one onto the launcher. Then, using a special gadget, he lit the fuse and stood back.

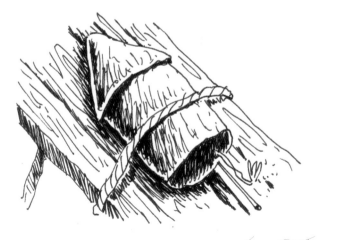

Stewie and the crowd of people in the pub garden gasped as they watched the first rocket swish its way high into the dark sky. Then, with a loud, thumping bang, it exploded in a huge flower of red and gold stars that hung in the air and then began to float gently down again and to fade away to darkness.

24

Stewie was spellbound. So many things he wanted to know all at once. Where did each star land? Where did the rocket shell end up? Did it burn away? What about the stout stick? So many important entries for his secret design book.

But here was Fred, straining to put the second rocket into the launcher.

Stewie Scraps counted six huge rockets hurtling into the sky above the pub garden. He saw colours and patterns that no school paints or felt-tips could ever capture.

And then it was all over.

Stewie tugged at Grandpa's sleeve. "Time to go home," he told him.

"What – already?" Grandpa looked disappointed.

But Stewie had to get back to his design book before certain special details faded from his head like the firework stars.

"Mum'll only worry. You know what she's like," he advised Grandpa. " She might even ring the pub to see where we are!"

He knew that would be too much for Grandpa – being checked up on by his own daughter!

"You're right, son," Grandpa agreed a little sadly, and tottered along the street with Stewie at his side.

"I really, really did have a good time, Grandpa," Stewie assured him.

"Me too," Grandpa said and tripped over the kerb.

Glues and screws and bits and bobs

On Saturday, 6th November, Stewie Scraps got up early and looked out the window. Another dull day. Perfect!

There would be lots of customers in the shop today, keeping Flo and JJ busy. Just what Stewie needed.

Stewie got dressed, grabbed some milk and biscuits for his breakfast and made his way outside. The yard was slightly damp, and there was a smell of burnt-out fires in the air.

At the end of the yard, he undid the shed lock and gently pushed open the rickety door.

The dull morning light filtered slowly into the shed. Stewie waited for the scuffling and scratching sound of Bugzy, his pet rat.

"Come on, sleepyhead," Stewie said. He bent down and lifted up the little white rat, holding him at face level. "We've work to do. Tonight, you and I are going to dance with the stars."

Bugzy twitched his whiskers and felt uncomfortable, though he couldn't say why.

It took Stewie a couple of hours to find all the bits that he needed for his Super Star Rocket. When no one was looking, he did a lot of hunting and searching in the shed, and in the yard outside. He crept about inside the shop amongst the boxes of old tools, toys, pots and pans, keeping away from his parents and the customers.

By late morning, however, he had laid out a selection of things of all shapes and sizes, ranging from a chunky, battered old broom handle to a thick metal tube.

It was time for the next part of his plan. And for that he needed secret access to JJ's glues-and-screws cupboard!

Stewie set himself a deadline for finishing his rocket — shop-closing time.

35

JJ liked to close at six on a Saturday. It gave the weekend bargain-hunters a little longer to browse.

It gave Stewie enough time to put the Super Star Rocket together.

He began his joining and fixing with great glee, pausing only once to return to the flat above the shop for a quick sandwich in the early afternoon.

Poppy was in the kitchen, eating vast amounts of cake and crying about the hairless boyfriend, who had ditched her last night. She had to find her own way home.

Flo was busying about trying to cheer her up.

By five o'clock, the Super Star Rocket, now aptly named the Stewie Scraps Super Star Rocket – or the

– was in more or less one piece.

Stewie climbed into the passenger pod, strapped himself in and then released the popping latch. The pod burst open and Stewie climbed out. He was completely satisfied with his day's work.

He checked his watch – 5.25pm. That gave him enough time to go back to the flat to assemble the down-suit before teatime, using some stretchy material he'd found in Flo's old sewing box.

Stewie pushed Bugzy towards his cage,

 tugged at the pull cord, and the shed and the SSSSR disappeared in the early November night. He pulled the rickety shed door closed behind him and stumbled back over the dark yard and into the back of the shop.

That night, Stewie asked to go to bed early.

"Are you feeling all right, dearie?" asked Flo. "Had a busy day," Stewie explained, truthfully. He chose not to mention the busy night ahead.

"Yeah — doin' nothin'," Poppy sneered. She seemed happier now. She dodged away from the cushion her little brother aimed at her.

But Stewie had no time for arguing.

Back in his bedroom, Stewie picked up the down-suit parts, stuffed a pillow under his duvet to make it look as if he was sleeping and stole quietly out the back door.

Up, up and away

Outside, a dull November moon hung about in the sky and a single rocket stuttered into the darkness. Stewie grinned.

Within the next few minutes, Stewie dragged the SSSSR out of the shed and heaved it into place in its rocket launcher by the back gate. Then, having put on the down-suit and reread his safety rules, he grabbed the struggling Bugzy and stuffed him into the front of the jacket.

"Tonight, my little friend, you will dance with the stars," Stewie reminded him, and together they climbed into the passenger pod.

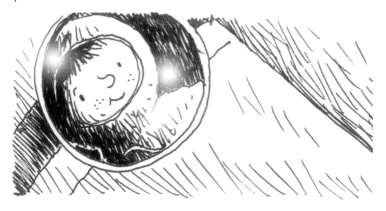

Bugzy looked up at the night sky and looked round the pod. He stared at Stewie in horror. Then he shot deep inside the down-suit. Stewie giggled.

"Hey! That tickles!" he said and wriggled in his pod seat. As he did so, he knocked a key-switch on the launchpad. The whole pod shook and groaned violently. Bugzy wriggled again inside the down-suit.

Stewie gasped.

The SSSSR crackled and fizzed in its launcher under him.

"Aaaah!" shrieked Stewie Scraps as the SSSSR screamed up out of its launcher, over the back-yard wall and right up into the November night.

When Stewie opened his eyes, the rocket was gathering speed. Stewie gulped and looked down.

The streets around JJ's shop were littered with tiny little bonfires where families were having their own bonfire parties. One or two rockets reached up from the ground below, like fingers of coloured sparks. Then they faded and died away.

None of them reached as high as the SSSSR, which continued its mighty climb above them all.

46

The air was filled with the smell of burning fireworks, a smoky, hazy smell that made Stewie's eyes water. But he knew he had to concentrate.

"Think hard, now," he told himself.

Somewhere deep inside the down-suit, Bugzy squeaked. And, for a moment, Stewie Scraps felt like squeaking, too.

The SSSSR, with Stewie and Bugzy aboard, sped on.

There was a lot of hissing and spitting that got steadily louder and then, just when Stewie thought he couldn't stand all the shaking and bumping any longer, the noises changed.

Suddenly, Stewie realized that the critical time was nearly here.

He closed his eyes and tried to remember what he had to do.

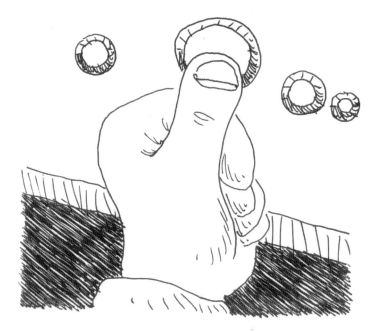

The rocket lurched, as it had reached its full height – and now it was about to explode.

Stewie opened his eyes and reached for the red key button – the one that looked like the top off a bottle of window cleaner.

He pressed for all he was worth.

The SSSSR passenger pod popped open like a big seed case and Stewie spun out into the darkness.

He felt the cold air on his face, rushing at him, pulling and tugging. Then two things happened more or less together.

The down-suit puffed out around him, inflating like a huge mushroom.

And, at the same time, there was a huge

The SSSSR exploded into thousands and thousands of tiny fire-petals that studded the black sky.

"Wow!"

Stewie was swinging gently away, going from side to side in the cold blackness. He looked around and it felt like he was in the middle of a huge, shimmering jewel.

CRACK

A second umbrella of silver and blue stars hung over his head. Stewie looked up into a dazzling brightness that seemed to follow him on his way down. He laughed and wiggled and flapped his feet.

Deep down in the down-suit, Bugzy wriggled, too.

"There you are, see," Stewie whispered. "Dancing with the stars, Bugzy. We're dancing with the stars."

And very, very slowly, they drifted down towards the ground.

Stewie hadn't put much thought into the landing. In the end, he found himself sitting on top of a bouncy castle. It had been put up for a charity fireworks party on the field a few streets away from JJ's shop.

The fireworks were over and the fire had died down now, but one or two children were still keen to bounce. The man who worked the castle was enjoying a last drink before packing up to go home.

"Oi!" The bouncy castle man had looked up and seen him. "How did you get up there? You're not allowed on there in fancy dress."

Stewie wanted to say: "I just swung down from the stars in my down-suit," but one look at the man's face told him it was not a good idea. He shrugged and grinned broadly, and, as quickly as he could, climbed down and raced back to the safety of JJ's shop.

Down to Earth with a bump

"Bloomin' kids!" JJ muttered. His ponytail swung angrily.

Stewie shrugged. "What's up?"

JJ pointed to a pile of wood near the gate, leaning up against the wall. It was charred and blackened as if it had been in a fire or had been part of a rocket-launcher.

Stewie gulped.

"Bloomin' kids," JJ muttered again, pulling at the wood and getting his hands black with soot. "Setting fire to the yard – throwin' fireworks around, no doubt. Well, I'll get 'em an' then there'll be trouble."

Stewie picked his way back to the shed and peered inside.

Grandpa was stroking Bugzy, who seemed none the worse for whatever had happened last night – kids, rockets, or whatever.

"Morning, Stewie."

"Hi, Grandpa."

"Wondered if you were looking for this?" Grandpa asked and pulled something from under the bench.

Stewie took it from him, slowly – the battered and blackened old tube that had been his SSSSR rocket case.

"A very special firework, I'd say," said Grandpa.

Stewie nodded.

"Found it the other side of the wall when I went for my paper. Always wondered where the main parts ended up, if they didn't get burned up," mused Grandpa.

"So did I, Grandpa," said Stewie. "So did I."

The End

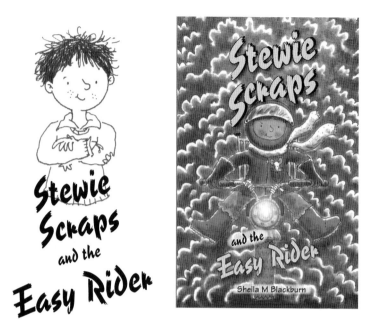

Stewie Scraps
and the
Easy Rider

Stewie's big brother Clint is always out with his friends on motorbikes.

"Oh, Wow! Come and look at this, Stewie!" calls Clint. It is a beautiful glistening red and chrome motorbike with long steering rods and long cow-horn handlebars!

Later that night, Stewie secretly flicks through Clint's bike magazines until he finds a picture of *that* bike. Then he does something really daring – he rips the page out of Clint's magazine.

Find out how Stewie builds his own bike and what happens on the Easy Rider's first outing.

Stewie Scraps and the Giant Joggers

Sheila M Blackburn

Stewie goes on an overnight school trip. It is his first time away from home and his first time in the countryside. His head is full of ideas for making this and making that.

Back at home, there's a surprise birthday party for Grandpa and a welcome home for Stewie.

Grandpa's present is a new pair of slippers. "Could you get me a new pair of legs to go with them?" he jokes.

In the dead of night Stewie sits bolt upright. He knows exactly what his next design is going to be.

Find out what Stewie builds and why he ends up in a mess of grass, leaves and twigs in the shed!

Stewie Scraps
and the
Trolley Cart

Sheila M Blackburn

Alfie Battersby, just about the cleverest and richest boy in Mr Melling's class, hands Stewie an invitation to his karting-party.

"Wow!"

Stewie is on Alfie's team at the karting track. He tries to remember everything he's been shown but it isn't as easy as he expects – and he isn't the only one having problems!

It is all over far too quickly.

Back at the flat, Stewie heads for the shed as soon as he can. "Got to get it all down before I forget." But his new design doesn't go according to plan. Find out what goes wrong and how Grandpa comes to the rescue.

Stewie Scraps and the Space Racer

Stewie spends all week wishing that Friday afternoon would come. It is "Art and Craft" on Friday afternoons, the only lesson Stewie willingly takes part in. When Mr Melling announces the start of a new project on space, Stewie knows exactly what to design, a spacecraft.

After school, Stewie rushes home with his prototype. He can't wait to build thereal thing. "We just need a few extra bits on the landing gear … and then … all systems go – tomorrow night," he tells Bugzy, his pet rat.

Find out where Stewie's Space Racer takes them and who he meets.

Stewie
Scraps
and the
Super Sleigh

Stewie Scraps
and the
Super Sleigh

Sheila M Blackburn

"Merry Christmas" reads a battered plastic sign in JJ's dusty shop window.

A new boy starts in Stewie's class and they soon become friends. Then Stewie realizes that since Miles came along, he hasn't come up with any new designs.

"That's it," he exclaims. "I've had an idea at last … . Perfect. Everything I need is here … . Look at my design" he tells Bugzy, his pet rat "The Stewie Scraps Super Sleigh … bet you can't wait!"

Stewie sits on the driver's seat of the sleigh … but nothing happens. He tries the next day and the day after that. Still nothing.

What's wrong with the sleigh? Why won't it go anywhere? What else does it need? Where will the Christmas Magic come from?